Ready to Be Royal

By *Valerie Tripp*
Illustrated by Thu Thai

★ American Girl®

Editorial Development: Teri Robida
Art Direction and Design: Jessica Rogers
Production: Caryl Boyer, Tami Heinz, Jodi Knueppel

? americangirl.com/service

Not all services are available in all countries.

Parents, request a FREE catalog at **americangirl.com/catalog.**
Sign up at **americangirl.com/email**
to receive the latest news and exclusive offers.

For Skylar Elizabeth Dawson
with love

The WellieWishers are a group of fun-loving kids who each have the same big, bright wish: to be a good friend. They love to play in a large and leafy backyard garden cared for by Willa's Aunt Miranda.

Willa

Ashlyn

Emerson

When the WellieWishers step into their colorful garden boots, also known as wellingtons or *wellies*, they are ready for anything—stomping in mud puddles, putting on a show, and helping friendships grow. Like you, they're learning that being kind, creative, and caring isn't always easy, but it's the best way to make friendships bloom.

Kendall

Camille

Bryant

Chapter 1

Curtsies, Crowns, and Bowing-Up-and-Down

One bright, brisk, blue-sky day, Camille said, "Let's pretend we're going to a school for fairy princesses and princes."

"That sounds like fun!" said Emerson. "You be our teacher, Camille."

"I'd love to," said Camille. She sang to the tune of "Twinkle, Twinkle Little Star":

Curtsies, bows, and magic, too!
How to make a wish come true!
Use a wand and cast a spell,
I'll teach you to do these well.
Come to school and learn to be
Ready to be royalty.

The WellieWishers held hands and chanted:

Close your eyes, stand in a row,
All hold hands, and off we go!

"Hello, students," said Princess Camille. "Welcome to Royal Academy!"

"Hooray!" said the students.

"Our first lesson is Curtsies, Crowns, and Bowing-Up-and-Down," said

Princess Camille. "Keep your chin up so that your crown stays steady. Watch me."

Princess Emerson liked curtsying. But she could *not* keep her crown straight!

She sang:

Curtsies are so fun to do!

But my crown needs magic glue!

Princess Emerson had a brainstorm. She tucked her pigtails *inside* her crown!

"Nice!" said Princess Camille. "Now you look royal!"

"Yes!" agreed Princess Kendall. "Way to use your head, Princess Emerson."

"Well, it's kind of *hair*-brained," laughed Princess Emerson. "But it works."

Everyone wore their crown in a goofy way. They sang:

Curtsies are so fun to do!

We can keep our crowns on, too!

"Okay!" laughed Princess Camille. "Enough *crowning* around. Come into the castle for our next lesson: Wands and Wishes!"

Chapter 2

Wands and Wishes

As the students sat down, Princess Camille handed out tote bags. "Look inside," she said, smiling.

"*Ooooh*," cooed Kendall. "A wand that's a pen, too!"

"I can't wait to use it," said Willa. She spun on one toe so that the star on her wand pen sparkled and glittered.

"Please take out your notebooks and pens," Princess Camille said.

Princess Camille pointed to the whiteboard. "Copy these spells in your notebooks," she said. "Next, try them out!"

Princess Willa was so excited! She wrote the spells so fast that the star on her wand pen was a blur.

Spells

To make wishes come true:
1. Wave wand three times.
2. Say, "Abracadabra! Cock-a-Doodle-Doo!
   Make this magic wish come true."

To undo a frog curse:
1. Wave wand twice.
2. Say, "You're a prince!"

Willa waved her wand. She read aloud what she had written in her notebook:

"To bake cow whiskers blue, say, 'Add a candelabra! Rock-a-poodle too! Make this magic wish come true."

Princess Willa had written so quickly that her handwriting was scribble-scrabble. When she read the first spell aloud, she got very funny results.

"Holy cow!" exclaimed Princess Willa. "Or I guess I should say *hairy* cow, because that cow has a big blue *moo*-stache! And why is that poodle in a rocking chair?"

Princess Willa tried the next spell, which was to undo a frog curse. When she read aloud what she had written in her notebook, the frog turned into all sorts of things.

A purse!

A pirate!

A prune!

"Ooops!" gasped Princess Willa. "I can't tell what I wrote. No wonder the frog is un*hoppy*!"

She sang:

Sometimes I just have to guess
'Cause my words are such a mess!

"I'm going to write the spells over again," said Princess Willa. "And this time, I'll write slowly and carefully."

When she was finished writing, Princess Willa read her spell.

Abracadabra! Cock-a-doodle-doo! Make this magic wish come true! You're a prince!

At last, Princess Willa turned the frog into a prince! "It took a while to rewrite the spells," she told the frog prince. "But it was worth it."

The frog prince smiled in agreement. Princess Willa sang:

When I did not rush to write,
My frog spell came out just right!

Chapter 3

Enchanting Animals

"Our next class is called Enchanting Animals," said Princess Camille. "Meet Princess Pegeen Piglet."

The students bowed and curtsied.

"Princess Pegeen is very smart," said Princess Camille. "If you talk to her, she'll answer you in her language. It's called Oinkish."

Would you like some tea?
Oink, oinky!
She said, Yes, please!
Can you fly?
Oink, oink-etty oinker!
She said, Yes, I can!

It's time for our riding lesson," said Princess Camille. "Meet Susie Unicorn."

"HOORAY!" shouted the students. They yelled so loudly that they startled Susie Unicorn. She skittered away.

"Please come back!" called Princess Ashlyn. But Susie Unicorn hid in the farthest corner of the paddock. No matter how much Princess Camille and the students called to her, Susie Unicorn would not come.

"I don't think Susie Unicorn will let us ride her," Princess Camille sighed. "Let's go back to the castle."

Princess Camille led the way, and all the students followed her eagerly.

Except Prince Bryant. "I'm shy sometimes, too, Susie Unicorn," he said softly. "I know how you feel."

Prince Bryant held out a daisy. He told Susie Unicorn a joke:

> *Knock, knock.*
>
> *Who's there?*
>
> *Wanda.*
>
> *Wanda who?*
>
> *Wanda eat a daisy?*

Susie Unicorn came to Prince Bryant and ate the daisy, tickling his hand with her soft nose. Prince Bryant stroked her nose and told her more jokes.

When the others came back, they were amazed to see Prince Bryant riding Susie Unicorn.

"Did you use magic to make Susie Unicorn change her mind?" asked Princess Camille.

"No," said Prince Bryant. "I wanted to make friends with her, so I told her jokes!"

Princess Camille laughed and sang:

Unicorns may run and hide;
Tell them jokes to get a ride!

Chapter 4

Crossing Moats and Climbing Towers

Yoo-hoo!" Princess Camille called. She waved from a window near the top of a tower.

Princess Ashlyn shuddered. "You're brave," she said. "I'm scared of heights."

"The next class is about crossing moats and climbing towers," said Princess Camille. "Use your brains and your magic to get Princess Pegeen and me down."

She sang:

Use your very best brainpower.

Cross the moat and climb the tower.

"Let's wish that we're fish," said Princess Willa, "and swim across."

"Let's jump to that stone!" said Princess Kendall.

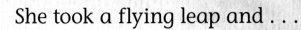

She took a flying leap and . . .

Ker-SPLASH! Princess Kendall fell into the moat.

Swoosh! Waves of water sloshed up onto the bank.

"Yikes!" yelled the other students. They jumped back to avoid getting soaked.

Princess Kendall sat up in the moat, spouting water.

"Are you all right?" asked Princess Ashlyn.

"Yes," said Princess Kendall. She laughed, "I'm all *wet*, too! I guess that wasn't a very royal thing to do."

"I don't want to splash down in my crown and gown," said Princess Emerson.

"You won't have to," said Princess Kendall. "Wait there."

Sloosh, slosh! Princess Kendall waded across the moat. She scrambled up the bank, crawling through the thick ivy that grew there.

Princess Kendall opened the door in the castle wall and then *crank, crank, crank*. She lowered the drawbridge.

As the students crossed the drawbridge, they said, "Thank you, Princess Kendall!"

"You're welcome!" said Princess
Kendall. Then she laughed and sang,
Next time that I cross a moat,
I sure hope I have a boat!

Princess Kendall pointed to the vines on the tower. "Who will climb up the ivy and open the window?" she asked.

"I'll do it," Princess Ashlyn offered.

"But you're afraid of heights," Princess Willa said kindly.

"I am," Princess Ashlyn admitted. "But I have to be brave if I want to be royal."

Princess Ashlyn took a deep breath. She tucked her wand into her sash. Then she put her foot on a tangle of ivy vines and *s-t-r-e-t-c-h-e-d* her arm out as far as it could go. Princess Ashlyn slowly climbed the ivy all the way up to the window. *Clink!* She lifted the latch. *Creak!* The window swung open.

Princess Ashlyn whisked her wand out of her sash, waved it, and said, "I wish we were birds. Abracadrabra! Cock-a-doodle-doo! Make this magic wish come true."

Swoop! The princess birds flew
down from the tower. Princess
Pegeen did, too.

Princess Emerson waved her wand and recited the spell to turn the birds back into princesses.

"Princess Pegeen and I both thank you for freeing us from the tower," said Princess Camille. "Now, follow me. I have a royal surprise."

Chapter 5

Prizes and Surprises

SURPRISE!" shouted Princess Camille. "It's time for a royal party!"

"HOORAY!" everyone cheered. They sang and danced and whooped it up. They ate delicious cookies, drank lovely tea, and had a wonderful time!

Then Princess Camille said, "Now it's time for prizes."

Tea Time

"Princess Emerson, you used your head *and* your imagination to solve the problem of your tippy, slippy crown. Good ideas can work magic. You win the Royal Creativity Award."

"I have a good idea for what to do with *this* crown," joked Princess Emerson, holding a crown cookie. "Eat it!"

"Princess Willa, you showed patience and determination when you rewrote your spells," said Princess Camille. "Stick-to-itiveness is magic. You win the Royal Award for Not Giving Up."

Princess Willa smiled. "The frog was pretty patient, too."

"Prince Bryant, you made friends with Susie Unicorn by telling her jokes," said Princess Camille. "It's magic to make people laugh. You win the Royal Award for Funniest Friend."

"Well," said Prince Bryant. "All I can say is:

Knock, knock.

Who's there?

Roy.

Roy who?

Royal Academy rocks!

"Princess Kendall, you really dove in to the challenge of crossing the moat," said Princess Camille. "You unselfishly helped the others, and that's the strongest magic of all. You win the Royal Kindness Award."

"Thank you!" said Princess Kendall, curtsying.

"You are afraid of heights, Princess Ashlyn," said Princess Camille. "But you climbed the tower anyway. Courage like that is pure magic. You win the Royal Award for Bravery."

"I'm just glad my fine-feathered-flying wishes came true," said Princess Ashlyn.

"We have a surprise for you, too, Princess Camille," said Princess Willa. "You win the Royal Award for Best Teacher *Ever*."

The students sang:

Curtsies, bows, and magic, too!

How to make a wish come true!

Use a wand and cast a spell,

You taught us to do these well.

Thanks to you we learned to be

Ready to be royalty.

"Go ahead!" said Princess Camille. "Unwrap your awards now."

The students unwrapped their prizes. "Ooh, look, it's a mirror!" they exclaimed.

"Turn it over," said Princess Camille. "What it says on the back is true. You are magical!"

you
are
magical

Learning Through Play

Playing school is a great way for kids to gain confidence as learners. Whether they're practicing real skills or making up their own, pretend play helps them prepare for the actual classroom experience. Taking on the role of the teacher can give your child a sense of control as she absorbs new information and rehearses school rules and routines. Here are some fun ways to encourage learning at home.

Create a classroom

Set up a space with a desk, mini chalkboard or dry-erase board, reading rug, books, and other school supplies. Have your child create a schedule that mirrors her own daily routine so she can practice transitioning from one subject to the next. Discuss classroom rules. Dolls and stuffed animals can stand in for your child's classmates!

Surprise subjects

Ask your child to create a class that she would like to take at school. What would it be called, and what would students learn? Maybe it's Slime Science, with hands-on experiments, or Talking to Turtles, with tips for communicating with animals.

Parents as students

Invite your child to teach you a skill. It could be something she's learned in school or preschool, a craft or hobby she enjoys, or a pretend skill.

Take turns

Taking turns is a school skill that often needs lots of practice. Help your child exercise patience by playing card or board games that require taking turns. Or make a game out of taking turns talking. Go clockwise around the dinner table or in the car, and give everyone a chance to speak without being interrupted.

Host a how-to video

Let your child pretend she's hosting a how-to video. Let her choose a task or an activity she enjoys, such as braiding hair, mixing cookie dough, or kicking a soccer ball. Record a video of her teaching step-by-step instructions. She'll have fun teaching and watching herself on camera.

Learn a new skill together

Take a class together. Whether it's in-person or online, learning a new skill with your child is a great way to show her that you're a student, too, and that learning lasts a lifetime.

About the Author

VALERIE TRIPP says that she became
a writer because of the kind of person she is.
She says she's curious, and writing requires you
to be interested in everything. Talking is her
favorite sport, and writing is a way of talking
on paper. She's a daydreamer, which helps her
come up with her ideas. And she loves words.
She even loves the struggle to come up
with just the right words as she writes
and rewrites. Ms. Tripp lives in
Maryland with her husband.